The Apocryphan

The Epifany of the Augusthog

by

D F Lewis

The Apocryphan
by D F Lewis

ISBN: 978-1-913766-18-4

Publication Date: July 2023

Copyright © 2012 by D F Lewis

Cover Art by David Rix, copyright 2023

www.eibonvalepress.co.uk

The Apocryphan

The Epifany of the Augusthog

I called myself the Summer Visitor but, if the truth were known, when I first arrived, Bonnyville was in its last ditch attempts to salvage its Summer season during an Autumn that, admittedly, was quite reasonably unseasonable. I think they called these periods Indian Summers in those days. This particular Indian Summer had extended itself beyond all conscience towards November.

Many of the rides and sideshows on the pier were already being boarded up by hairy men who had now apparently become less customer-orientated, especially in their use of language. As I proceeded further along the promenade, I saw some parked dinghies and yachts, their rigging-ropes loudly snapping in the sea-breeze against the masts with a rhythm that matched my stride. I then saw a middle-aged man throw some crumbs from his bag on to the beach and a swarm of gulls wheeled above waiting for both of us to reach a distance: a shorter and shorter distance as they grew more frantic and foolhardy. It was a wild scribble of wings in the lower sky that was almost frightening. But I was strangely aware their noise was rather muted, in contrast to the tangled configurations of pounce and dive.

I decided to walk further along the coast, away from the seasonal attractions towards a more residential area. Simultaneously, the sun was greyed over by mist, making it a dull gold coin above the sea's horizon. It reminded me of the true end-of-season gloom that such resorts as Bonnyville would normally boast at this time of the year. I watched a portly lady get out of a car and waddle in evident pain with her large hips swinging slowly from side to side as she crossed, with a heavy Tesco bag in each hand, through a bungalow's garden towards its door.

I returned to the more touristy end of town, determined to become the Summer Visitor I knew myself, at heart, to be. Just because I was late did not change the nature of my identity.

As I headed towards the pier, I found a small group (locals not visitors) around a makeshift fresh wet-fish stall on the lower promenade. The floppy and the slimy all thrown together on a couple of trestle-tables leant against by crudely chalked backboards indicating prices.

Nearby, despite the lateness of the season and the disappearance of most children schoolward, there was the playful blue train that travelled the lower promenade giving pointless return journeys. Today, it had one paying passenger on board (the middle-aged man of the bird-crumbs) as it started its outward trip. No doubt, a few weeks ago, there had been active queues for such a jaunt.
It was probably its last journey of the season.

I waved to the young woman behind the steering-wheel. She looked odd in the undersized train-cab, one that travelled on tyred wheels like a car… pulling the carriages behind it, between the line of beach huts and the beach. She waved back. As did the passenger. As if we all had been fast friends for years.

I hopped on—as an impulse—towards the back.

As the 'train' trundled in the direction from which I had just returned, I thought back over the many regular years I had been the Summer Visitor. In the early days, I had been accompanied by my late husband. We had been an inseparable couple: a pair of Summer Visitors, now down to just one. A couple of Bonnyville trippers. Now, as I say, just one. Perhaps two in spirit.

The 'train' was only due to travel two miles along the lower promenade, before turning upon a concrete 'winding-hole' where one could alight at a seasonal café or just go back again straightaway! For most of the journey, the sea was hidden from view by a high concrete barrier. The sea's own 'fire-wall' in the modern parlance, except I imagined it easily breachable, given the thrust of nature. The journey reminded me of life itself.

Thinking of my husband again, I remembered how his very companionship had seemingly thwarted all dangers. Lying in bed awake, with him snoring beside me, I knew I was safe. But, even then, at the back of my mind, I'm sure I knew if there was a cataclysmic storm or nuclear attack or whatever, I'd be no more safe under the covers of that psychologically protective bed within his arms, than I would anywhere else or with anyone else. However, even *that* thought became as pointless as this 'train' journey, for we are all passengers on this planet, our togetherness being no protection against premature or sudden death. No protection, indeed, against *natural* death.

As I watched the backs of the heads of the driver and the bird-crumb man from my perch in the last carriage, I was disturbed by their air of innocence; their apparent inability to forget the happiness of the moment … too entrenched in or entranced by their escapism of activity. Shaking off such observations, I wondered if I'd be forced to buy a ticket for the journey, having hopped on at the last moment. It was very cheap to buy a ticket, bearing in mind the basic nature of the short featureless journey. But I had a sudden rush of daredevilry when I prepared to hop off again just as quickly, just as gratuitously, so to speak.

A huge low shape passed abruptly overhead towards the sea, sensed as only missing my head by a few feet. Its shadow quickly spread like disease around us, but vanished just as quickly. You would have expected screaming jet engines. But the thing silently met the waves creating a fountain fit for the major attraction in a magnificent modern city. I had not seen whatever it was full on. Only the results. And it was then that real screaming did ensue, if belatedly. Making me forget what I had not seen.

I was too old to be the Summer Visitor, they said. Too wrinkled, too old-fashioned, and (not to put too fine a point on it) 'past it'. More likely, however, the season itself had suddenly changed at the very point of my regular visit that year, causing me to vanish from view in actual transit. It is a commonly unknown fact that the Summer Visitor cannot exist when Summer has ended. Bonnyville was now ready—an empty slate—for a tale of off-season romance and of things I would never know about. The state of the weather was neither here nor there. It was just the turning-point of the seasons that counted.

The train swung slowly round its turning-point. The bird-crumb man got off to have a coffee at the café.

Two Tesco bags sat on the kitchen table, their contents either crackling or melting. The lady who had carried them in was slumped against the fridge. Slipped there like a plump wet-fish. Luckily her size had broken the fall. Tears were in her eyes. A deep noise vibrated the floor for a few seconds. A common experience in Bonnyville, as the Government regularly tested heavy-duty explosives at an army site not far away on the nearest coast just beyond the sea's horizon. Nobody local noticed such sounds any more. Only visitors.

The sound of snapping from upstairs kept to its tight rhythm. That was her husband practising. She called to him to help get her up.

○

The bird-crumb man finished his coffee. There were not many visitors today. All the Summer ones had long since returned to their homes. He was probably the only visitor to Bonnyville today. That was because he was the Winter Visitor. Proud of it, too. Not many were given the calling over the years. He noticed a shape slumped on a nearby beach, topped by a querulous gull. The 'train' was on its return journey by now and the café staff at the back preparing to shut up shop, perhaps forever. The bird-crumb man got up, sat down again, fingered his mobile, then decided to investigate. His mind was a scribble of wings.

○

Nobody missed the Summer Visitor. It had been a bad Summer, when push came to shove. Rained off most of the time, even on Air Show day ... that day of otherwise so many potential visitors.

Bonnyvilleans went about their Winter business, deaf to the sound of the odd paramedic siren. Deaf, too, to the rhythm of their own footsteps. Blind to the pier. Blind even to the sea itself. Nobody noticed anything. They did not even watch for traffic, when they crossed the road.

The last train from Bonnyville Terminus hooted mournfully into the encroaching night. A real train on real tracks. Nobody left, because nobody had come.

Q

Many first encountered the Apocryphan in the form of an iconic Red Indian figurehead embedded within—or merely stuck upon – a brick wall near a back entrance in a side street. It was often embossed upon an ornate door of an arcade shop, even in a main thoroughfare—an icon that aprocryphised itself time and time again. Unnoticed, although recorded here.

There was an Apocryphan in a road opposite Bonnyville pier, erected upon a bricked-up door-opening that had once been the entrance to a fish shop (a baguette shop in more recent years). This particular 'Red Indian' was a statue or sculpture with a smooth hard mineral-looking skin of a wonderful shining deep blue. Its head-dress was of multicoloured feathers ... an inscrutable expression on its face, with most of its body sunk into the brickwork, but still visible as a recognisable body. The left arm was invisible behind its back. But in its right hand could be seen a hand of standard playing-cards, splayed in a fan, as if ready to play.

Like most icons, religious or not, this blue Apocryphan became barely noticed over the turning years, if noticeable at all. Bonnyvilleans—during the seemingly endless Winter seasons— trudged past it on their various duties of survival, with not a single side glance. The *sense* that they knew it was there, however, remained as powerful as ever.

◌

Adrian entered a watch shop on the other side of Bonnyville, near the caravan site. He had left his watch to be repaired. There had been a fill-in watchmaker who had accepted his watch for repair, because the real watch-shop owner was on holiday. Adrian remembered his watch being put on a back shelf.

Today, the real watch-shop owner had returned.

"I've come to collect my watch. I left it on Thursday." Adrian was not a typical Bonnyvillean. He was someone you might see on TV anywhere. He could have been quite a personable host, given the opportunity. Not bad looking. He had even missed wearing his watch with a feeling of empty wrist. He noticed his watch wasn't where it had been put on the back shelf.

"Hmmm, Thursday… I wasn't here then." The shopkeeper was brusque, obviously embarrassed about something.

"I know you weren't. Your colleague took my watch in."

"He was holiday relief. He took the watches away to mend."

"You mean he stole them?"

Shrugs.

"I can let you have another watch." He opened a cabinet of new watches.

"You can have this one for £6.50." He showed a particularly nice gold watch with a sweeping second hand. Much nicer than Adrian's own watch.

There was a gasp of astonishment from other customers queuing behind Adrian.

Adrian decided to cut his losses and quickly paid over the £6.50. Based on the comments of the other customers, Adrian had realised that the proffered watch was worth a lot more than £6.50. He left the shop with a shop-door 'ding!', while threading his wrist into the new watch, with some pride of possession. Every cloud has a gold lining, he thought.

◌

When it rained in Bonnyville it almost rained forever. Storm-rods created 'dancing fairies' on the pavements and roads … and deep dimples in the sea. Sweeping across the promenade like over-egged stage-effects being splashed into actors' faces from the wings. Old-fashioned TV similitudes of soaking being splashed, too, by over-eager technicians from behind the camera. Bonnyville, however, was no black-and-white film-set. It really existed. It really was that way.

Adrian heard the rain hissing in his ears in competition with the tides and with his own tinnitus. He suffered the teeming tides of the sky to inundate him as first cousins to the sea's own tides. Tides of windblown Autumn leaving for Winter. No lingering memory of the Summer Visitor. No hope even for a *new* memory of the Summer Visitor anytime soon. Just the tidings of the present moment, a moment that lasted forever, as drenched by delay. An ever-resisting delay.

Adrian glanced at his new watch to check its moment … its movement. Wondering briefly if it was water-proof or merely water-resistant. Wonder turning to worry without even the moment turning to the next moment. The turning-point of moments that never seemed to click into position.

For a Bonnyvillean, he was uncharacteristically optimistic. Pro-active. Able to match moment with moment, given the chance. Given the luck. But there was not much luck in Bonnyville, he knew. The watch had stopped.

There was ever the feeling that one was wading through a treacle of resisting destinies. Or if not treacle, certainly a cloying mass of defeatism, of bending before what the weather brought as well as a deep-seated anxiety about making any decisions within such a pointless environment of unpredictability and sloth.

Adrian reached the end of the pier. He faced the sea with equanimity. He couldn't possibly get any wetter. He threw the watch into a soaring then diving arc as it disappeared into the spume and spray of an invisible darkness, a darkness disguised by the growing promise of dawn, laced with white foam upon prematurely light-refracted raindrops.

He glimpsed down at his feet. The sodden boardwalk of the pier—close to where the fishermen would later that day congregate in their wet gear—was glimmering into a shape beneath his shoes that Adrian's teardrop or raindrop eyes could barely discern. But he managed to see the knotty configuration of a pig-like face in the wood's grainy fibre, as made proud by decades of scuffing from visitors' Summer sandals.

He ran and ran back to the land, till he could run no further, believing that the pier extended itself even as he ran.

○

The woman lifted the lid from the butter dish. Another gyrning face grooved into its yellow surface. Her husband always waited for a new block of butter to be installed before creeping down in the night with his penless pen-top ready to score out another utterly butterly grimace. She'd only bought the butter today at the supermarket. He must have done it when she was in the loo. In contrast, the milk often went so bad—between shopping trips—that it made its own faces in the pungent curds settled at the bottom of the jug.

She waddled to the fridge—hips too wide to go one way and not the other between the kitchen table and the kitchen walls—in order to replace the butter-dish on its inside door-slot shelf, having taken care to smooth out its yellow surface with the back-bone of her comb. She was perturbed to see that the carrots were fresh off a popular TV programme demonstrating vegetables that had grown naturally into strange humorous recognisabilities of shape. And the plastic packaging of next Sunday's roast was bottom-sized, its translucency vaguely revealing a pinkish cartilage or hen-wing between the cheeks. A shapely bottom. Unlike her own body's half an acre of blotched hams-on-the-bone.

She shut the fridge door with a sigh as she contemplated yet another ascent of Everest represented by the stairs to the bedroom in the bungalow's roof.

○

The Sixpenny Queen was Adrian's local. He had decided that nightmares were more bearable than real life. He managed to wring a living from the local streets of this coastal enclave by working in Benefits for the poor, needy and those who thought themselves poor or needy. Disabled in some way. Some disabled by the belief that they were disabled when they were not. Office work was a doddle, especially when you were only there, Adrian thought, to carry out the instructions of others and not think.

Claura worked behind the bar at *The Sixpenny Queen*. Adrian quite liked her. She had something about her beyond the run-of-the-mill. Attractive in an acquired taste sort of way. She also did the ultimate barmaid's job, by cheering up the punters, making them believe she was flirting with each of them, but only acting when she was seen flirting with others.

The Sixpenny Queen was an old pub, a traditional large one with decorated mirrors and flock wallpaper, not decked out as a multiplex-with-food, but genuinely a nineteen-thirties drinking-hole for when locals had little else to do come the evenings.

Today, Adrian leaned on the bar—staring at his bare wrist. Then staring at the shapely bottom of Claura as she served a stranger-to-town by the look of him. She even acted flirtations with strangers, Adrian thought. No shame.

○

Seen from above, the blue Apocryphan stood out from its fixture in the wall around the doorway of the derelict shop, its feathers prominent beyond the edge of slate roof that hid a lot of the rest of it.

Standing even higher than the slate roof was a position upon Bonnyville's war memorial. Three people stood on the brink of falling, where it was believed the *possibility* of falling was tantamount to falling itself, giving each of the trio the irresistible urge simply to jump. None of the three could quite work out which one of the three he or she was. Desperately trying to keep the balance of mind and body together. Falling or jumping, it little mattered, as either would result in certain death.

Or waking.

Nobody could be sure.

Another (a fourth) stood, in a similar state of indecision, upon the disintegrating peak of a huge slagheap that threatened to collapse upon Bonnyville school. The only difference between the heap and the memorial was that the former was not a known feature of Bonnyville, whilst the latter was indeed the town's sole landmark when viewed from a distance (as from a pirate radio station floating at sea beyond territorial waters or a helicopter lost between its departure point and destination).

Adrian's brother, Charlie Bubbles, put the flat black vinyl disc of a David McWilliams song on the 45 rpm spinning padded bakelite 'plate'. So much more professional than his Dansette autochange of his recent youth. He squawked a few pointless words over the Winter airwaves. Introductory jabber above a competing jingle about Radio Caroline and its current sponsor.

Bulova Watches, meanwhile, told the time at the head of each hour. The news was brought by courtesy of ripping off the BBC. The turntable itself was cushioned by shock absorbers to absorb the shock of the waves. The real waves. The ship's transmitter mast, even on a relatively calm day like today, swung quite a distance from the true as well as the magnetic vertical between the slow-sloping horizons of the North Sea.

Charlie looked through the grimy window of his musical cockpit and knew that one of his horizons was the sight of Bonnyville upon the nearest coast. Its war memorial stuck up like a wounded thumb. He wondered how Adrian was getting on. Spent most of his days in the 'Sixpenny Queen'. Charlie shrugged. They had travelled to Bonnyville, both with the ambition to become Disc Jockeys on the new-fledged army of pirate stations that were at that time setting up. But only Charlie had made the grade with his 'gift of the gab'. Charlie was a man of communication's massive future. Adrian had always been the more churlish, the more taciturn of the two. So, Adrian had to resort to merely being part of the supply chain for the radio station's catering. He rowed the boat of provisions to and from the shore. When he wasn't drinking or mouching on the pier or eyeing Claura's backside, that is.

Even at this very moment, Adrian gazed out of the pub's window towards the sea and the tiny silhouette of the single tall-masted ship against the darkening sky … at the same time as Charlie looked out of his own cockpit window during the teatime show. Their two unconscious gazes met across the sea. Adrian turned towards the only other customer in the pub. The Winter Visitor. A man whose trouser turn-ups were stacked with bread crumbs.

○

As the Winter months unfolded from one to the other, seemingly endlessly, the forest of tall single-masted ships gathered momentum in the East, making this section of the coast a force-field of tangled programming, mixing Stones with Yardbirds. Indeed, eventually, the radio ship on which Charlie had been based was forced to travel many miles round the coast to a North Western area with the intention of pioneering offshore radio within the tarry waters of Black Pool. Before it departed, Charlie had transferred to a rival ship, as he didn't want to leave his kid brother Adrian alone in the Bonnyville area. Or that was the reason he gave himself at the time. So soon forgotten.

Adrian still rowed the boat to and fro. The weather was counter-productive and, often, the sea-sick disc-jockeys were left abandoned for weeks at a time. The rock-music hit parades were kept afloat by sheer grit and determination. And ambition.

Adrian was struck by nothing. He had ceased to be that care-free, confident lad he had once been before coming to Bonnyville, one with far more natural gumption than those drinking-friends with whom he mixed in the 'Sixpenny Queen'. He hadn't always been the morose taciturn individual that Bonnyville had turned him into. Charlie had soon ceased to recognise him. And vice versa.

Charlie had become a big noise. Charlie Bubbles: now a household name in the transmission area of the radio ship. And beyond. He never wanted to go on shore leave, because he needed to forge ahead with his show business ambitions of celebrity, perhaps with a future TV chat show on the horizon (given the strength of fantasy and imagination). He was always on the air. Often standing-in for John Peel during the small hours in the Perfumed Garden. A workaholic. A ship-freak.

Adrian had his own erstwhile liveliness sucked out by the persona of Charlie Bubbles. Not a half-brother, but a whole one. As if Charlie was a celebrity vampire: feasting on the profile of his kid brother, whilst also lowering the profiles of all those who listened to him or of visitors to the ship with whom he came into contact.

These visitors left as lesser mortals ... careering up and down in the sluggish dinghy, as they prepared (inside their heads) journalistic copy on Charlie Bubbles for the next edition of New Musical Express.

○

The town of Bonnyville—now unseen from the top of the war memorial where no dare-devil had climbed for ages (given the increasingly cowed quality even of the town's callow youth)—had within its overall pattern of streets and buildings gained the easily imagined configuration of a snouted face. And, unseen, too, the radiant blue 'skin' of the Apocryphan's extended arm holding a fanned hand of trump cards towards blinkered passers-by.

Perhaps the memorial itself was a sort of radio transmitter, broadcasting mind-crushing gloom, unmixed by any popular music of the times. Unrelieved by bubbly chatter between the black vinyl tracks.

○

"Apocryphan, Apocryphan, who art thou, Apocryphan?"

The whole town of Bonnyville sat silent in the uncharacteristically crackling electricity of a Winter storm. Jagged yellow streaks crawled along the sea's furthest horizon like creatures seeking a nightmare to inhabit.

Reflected in the glow, the Blue Indian managed to pocket the hand of playing-cards before getting wet. The eyes glanced up—from their stone sockets—at the War Memorial while recalling only a few weeks before when many old soldiers (some in wheelchairs or motorised buggies) had grouped around its base on Remembrance Day. Remembrance of Things Past. Each proudly sporting a poppy. So red, only dreams could make them *that* red.

Tonight represented the tail-end of the wreaths that had been laid earlier: gloomy on a warm day in November, commemorating and celebrating the bravery of the seaside resort's past inhabitants. One such wreath—with at least a single still vibrant bloom completing its circle of interwoven growth—crawled towards the Remembrance Gardens to seek its missing roots. Genealogy gone native.

○

Rain drummed heavily on the roof directly above his head. The man stared at the blood-spill on his bedside table. It was not real. It was one of those makeshift mementoes that crinkled in the fingers like a crepe-paper poppy. He heard his wide knicker-bockered wife in the room below stowing the week's shopping in the fridge. Then, amid grumbles from unseasonal thunder, he heard her gasp and then slump to the linoleum as the storm reached a level akin to God's removal men dropping one of His heavier sticks of furniture from Heaven to Hell.

The man decided not to investigate. He started snapping his braces against his chest in a relentless attempt to match the rhythm of his own heart. He swallowed hard. He knew he would feel guilty forever at not feeling guilty at all about not venturing downstairs to help his ailing wife. She would get up soon enough and continue tidying things up. Unless she had broken a hip. Or a chest of drawers.

The old couple's chalet bungalow was only one mere step from becoming a house, given its potential ability to turn integral eaves-cupboards into separate independent wardrobes. Its whole nineteen-thirties built structure jumped as each thump crumpled on its door from a hand softened by the collapsibility of card-fingers.

○

Despite the higher than average seasonal temperature, it did snow during that everlasting winter. A slight crystal carpet crackled underfoot accompanied by tantalising fairy crepitations in the air so unlike the earlier grumbling thunder of the Winter's earlier stages. Adrian wandered with a lighter heart than usual, speculating on how quickly the snowy settlings of frost would become yellow slush.

The distant masts of the derelict radio-ships still criss-crossed in moving patterns of fencing duels in a light breeze that brought more frost particles with it—cascades of precipitation straight into Adrian's face like invigoratingly cool acid drops. His brother Charlie Bubbles was now a Member of Parliament, vying for the Prime Minister's job. Charlie Bubbles, or Charles Paliser as he now called himself.

Paliser was Adrian's family name, too, of course, but rarely used in the conflicting associations that constituted the anonymous seaside communes of drinkers, drug-pushers and simpletons. Charlie had evidently forgotten Adrian or had turned a blind eye or deaf ear whenever resistance towards Charlie's own attempts at remembrance was visited upon him by the self-satisfied exigencies of guilt. Adrian had never even attempted to remember Charlie so it was far more difficult to forget.

○

The depth of Winter—as it had now become—was when the Winter Visitor most easily thrived, unthwarted by any propinquity of thaw. He gathered stale bread from the white-frosted dustbins and minced it with his fingers into coagulants of crumb. Then fed the ill-squawking gulls with a frenzy that matched beaks with human brain. They often swirled above him like one large haphazard construction of air, feather and bone.

One particular dustbin the Winter Visitor rifled was outside a chalet bungalow with two dormer windows set into its roof like protruding eyes. There was very little to find. No rubbish, mixed or unmixed with recyclings of better rubbish. Only items of clothing and disposable Tesco carrier-bags. He shrugged. Often returning to see if he believed his own eyes. Only reason to mention this dustbin at all.

☉

Claura still worked behind the bar at *The Sixpenny Queen*. She was a little thicker at the waist, heavier at the bosom and longer at the hair. None of it grey. She was just as colourful as her still well-honed charms of flirtation continued to attract the similarly aging customers. The whole town aged.

"Staring into your beer again?" she said to one whose name she'd never got right. "What you see there? A face?" She laughed. Laughing off the face that often showed incipient wrinkles depending which mirror she chose to look in. And there were plenty in the lounge bar.

"It's just that it's not my own face," answered the man with no name, having grown out of being called Adrian, because being forgotten by his brother had made him forget himself. He was no longer anyone's brother. Drained even of that profile.

He prayed for the return of August and its seasonal jobs on the pier.

He looked back at the surface of his beer where the specific gravity had sucked the nose wider, rounder and the eyes smaller, beadier and the cheeks into jowls or wattles or dewlaps.

"What's the time?" he asked.

Claura looked up at the large pub clock. She did not reply.

○

Midwinter in the area of the world where Bonnyville is situated is generally considered to be January 18th, taking into account the positioning of the Christmas period (e.g. light-scarcity syndrome relief, some light heartedness factors of Yuletide etc.) and the various average weightings of weather conditions throughout the centuries, plus some astrological harmonics far more complex than any mere Sun Sign considerations that popular newspapers published.

On that day during the particular longueurs of the Winter in question, a man, dressed as a bedraggled Santa Claus, staggered through a snowstorm, a remarkably heavy one bearing in mind the relatively high average temperature of the earlier stages of the season. He was still dressed as Santa Claus because he found himself with no other clothes to wear after disporting himself in *The Sixpenny Queen* for a children's party a few weeks before.

He had been trying to re-locate the chalet bungalow with the sartorially generous dustbin outside it … but—despite knowing Bonnyville like the back of his hand—he had not exactly recalled the directions of reality or dream that had first led him there as the Winter Visitor. Even when he had been Adrian Paliser, as opposed to the Visitor, there had been doubts as to the sense of his own direction or as to the provenance even of a forgotten person with only an inch of profile left in his dimpled pint-glass.

Claura had only given him a merest glance as he left the pub with undignified haste, having been found with no presents in his sack, only junk mail he hadn't yet delivered.

Becoming Adrian somehow prevented him from being the Winter Visitor any longer—even masquerading as such—because he had been in Bonnyville too long. His sojourn had even outlived the Prime Minister's long-fought parliamentary Marine Offences Act that had served to denude the high seas of all radio-ship masts.

Perhaps, after all, Adrian and the Visitor were quite separate existences.

He suddenly stumbled into a strange area of town where he had perhaps been before which, with some paradoxical stretching of the truth into wishful thinking, meant he might now rediscover the chalet bungalow. Instead, the roads didn't look right except for fulfilling the slightly more relaxed rules of partial recognition. One alley was yards from where it should be. One bungalow chimney had three aerials instead of one (heavy-duty aerials tantamount to full-blooded transmitters rather than simple aids to receiving terrestrial TV). As Santa Claus, he rather despised all chimneys in modern times, as they seemed blocked either at top or bottom— or both. Junk mail rather than soot.

Indeed, there was one completely new ginnel that separated two rows of terraced houses and their outside toilets by a mere few yards of cobbles, now stacked with fresh dusk-stained snow in the shape of crystallised bread-crumbs. He laughed at his own conceit.

Down this ginnel he found parked the blue 'train' that—during the Summer months—gave rides along the lower promenade. He had often wondered where it was kept in the off-season. Common sense meant it had to be somewhere. So why not here?

He remembered Claura's words in his mind as he walked along its snow-strewn length:

"They bloody plonk that train-ride thing at the back of my house during the winter! I'm sure it breeds rats by the sound of it. Sure it's not really allowed to be there…"

At the time, he had only half-listened to her 'pub talk'. He rarely listened properly any more to anyone. He only nodded and asked the time.

As he passed beside the train, on that fateful 18th day of January, a frost-bitten hand suddenly stuck out from one of the carriages and offered him a hand. The back of it was fanned out like interleaved mock marble or flock wallpaper or mosaic laws.

○

Dr Dumond sat back in his surgery. As one of the few medical practitioners in Bonnyville, he saw all sides of life: the benefit claimants, the seasonal workers, the inbred locals, the rumour-mongers, the few aspirant traders, the commuters, but especially the ill, the thought-to-be-ill and the thought-to-be-dead-or-dreaming.

His grim carved face reflected the shadow of a moment's thought. Was he, too, indeed, one of the dreamers he treated with pills? He stared through the window at a small low-flying aircraft, almost toy-like with its over-sized propeller at the front and the squat wings: its fuselage made from heavy-duty wickerwork fit for a laundry-basket. It buzzed over the War Memorial then disappeared across the empty sea in an unknown direction, because Dr Dumond had blinked at the precise moment it disappeared from view.

His dusky looks were ever out of place in Bonnyville. But being the nearest to a lynch-pin of health that the inhabitants would ever possess, he was treated with a grudging respect. He sneered silently as he heard his receptionist opening the waiting-room door to the troops of the crestfallen and the malingering. He had forgotten his own pills that reminded him to take them in the first place. Doctors needed more pills than most people just to keep them sane, in the face of human deprivation and disease. Most of them hid this weakness behind sartorial elegance and stern diffidence. And a cosmetic necklace shaped like a stethoscope.

Laurence Dumond never wore a watch. That seemed to help. Have you noticed doctors never wear watches?

○

The voiceover was clear. Prime Minister Paliser was making an important announcement on the radio, interspersed with old Sixties records which he introduced jauntily between the gravitas. His speech concerned the huge landfill waste piles that had increasingly appeared all over the country, as there was no more land to fill. Huge soggy muckpiles or cobbled slagheaps of Winter-darkened incombustibles. One even darkened the north side of Bonnyville, near the junior school. The playground never got the sun even in the days of the Summer Visitor.

Adrian fiddled with his earpiece to catch his brother's words more clearly—except he no longer knew them as his brother's. They were insidious grumbling shades of communication on the edge of importance but never quite reaching beyond into the cognitive consciousness. The musical interludes were 'Hats Off To Larry' by Del Shannon, 'Without You' by Johnny Tillotson, 'Kommotion' by Duane Eddy, 'Rubber Ball' by Bobby Vee, 'The Hog' by William Hope Hodgson and 'Let There be Drums' by Sandy Nelson.

The small aircraft returned across the town from the direction of the sea and circled the slagheap, evidently surveying the problem. Adrian threw some breadcrumbs around him, as if expecting it to land at his feet.

The snow had disappeared within the last few days—and a hopeful Spring was hovering in the air. He now slept in the blue 'train' most nights, having been thrown out of his bedsit near the pier. Watching out for Claura. And playing Patience.

○

The classroom was quite dark. Year Five was in session. Mr Socrates should have switched the lights on. But that was no different in the Summer. Last Summer they received an Ofsted visit, one that noted the problem with lighting as part of its inspection report. That seemed ages ago now. Nothing had been done. He shrugged. He surveyed the ranks of faces staring up at him, open-mouthed. Some were as dark as the darkness that surrounded them—the six Dumond children, offspring of the new local doctor. Most of the others were Paliser faces or relatives of the Palisers, a long-term family of Bonnyville, whose miscegenations Mr Socrates had long since ceased to fathom. Yet they were pure English to the furthest diminishing skyward roots of their genealogical tree.

Many names made calling the register a problem, until he invented a fail-safe method of checking attendance, the intricacies of which are beyond our current remit.

The faces remained open-mouthed. They had just heard an aircraft buzzing over the school followed closely by an enormous crash in the vicinity. Mr Socrates himself was shocked but he managed to calm the children down. They heard distantly wailing sirens. There was no clear view through the windowlene-smeared windows.

"Don't worry, children I'm sure there's a simple explanation." Except not simple enough for him to have explained it to himself. And he shook his long locks in his customary manner or tic. His lined face revealed his age. Not laugh-lines, but frown ones. The remains of a tragic youth and bereft accomplishments. "Carry on with your drawings."

"Mine's a painting!" piped up one boy, sitting next to Denise Dumond in a double-desk.

He held up a blue image of a barely discernible human shape with a head of feathers.

"That's nice," said Mr Socrates, absent-mindedly. It reminded him of a stain he'd seen on the wall when last inspecting the Boys toilet. Disinfectant misfired by a careless council cleaner, he'd assumed.

"Mine's a drawing of you," said Denise, having evidently decided her work was better than her neighbour's. She held up a very carefully sketched depiction of the fish stall near the pier, complete with a very characterful treatment of the stallholder holding up a long snoutfish (a local catch) of which he was just as proud as Denise was of the drawing she had, in turn, held up.

"That's not me, is it? It looks like Mr Smee the fishmonger. But it is rather good. I'll put it on the wall."

Denise—a tall girl for her age, even when sitting down—turning her drawing round to look at it, said: "Ah, yes, sorry. This one is of you, Sir." And she held up another one which was rather an abstract design: a very kind way to describe scribble.

Mr Socrates looked at his watch.

With the noise of the crash forgotten, they even forgot they had forgotten it, to the extent it probably never happened at all. Meanwhile, school business went on, and reports written, parents seen and unseen wandering the corridors ready to complain at the slightest matter, the headmaster in his study studying the huge pile of rubbish that seemed to approach the school day by day, cobble by cobble, yester-egg by yester-egg, vinyl platters, moist residues of forgotten dinners, anthracite nuts that would never burn, tails of animals whose owners would never miss them, disused card-games fingerprinted by decay … and Year Five's drawings and paintings accidentally unrecycled to the paper waste, equally foxed by the mystery of entropy.

○

The air was cold, despite there being a sense of Spring in the air. The tops of the waves cut the lower layer of warm interleaved tissue laid across them as if in preparation for an outlandish piece of modern artwork stretching from coast to coast, similar to a full-scale mountain being wrapped in red crepe paper as a giant 'happening'.

Adrian kicked his feet along the beach. He was ever on the look-out for the Summer Visitor's return but, so far in the changing pattern of the season, with very little hope of seeing her. He scattered bread-crumbs in his wake as if a Hansel leaving a trail for his Gretel. He did not notice the scarcity of gulls. None flew down to misdirect the carefully laid plans or pathways of mankind. He watched the sun set through gossamer lenses refracting the billowing imaginations of tissue and spray-tossed tides. Paradoxically a brighter red the darker it became.

He saw the skeletal ghost of his brother's radio station craning to pick the sea's horizon from the ground like a girder.

They had cleared the oceans of rubbish. Not even boats were allowed to ply the channels between the ports and mooring-places. So now, at least, there were expanses of view uncluttered by anything man-made. Adrian had only to turn on the balls of his feet to witness the obverse side of that coin. Government-licensed sites of waste heaping the coast like Hodgsonian redoubts. Hopping across the land with real corruptions of art, each happening opening, each opening happening, jerking out, like vomit, each gruesome grind and under-slime to become a camouflage of both town and landscape in the shape of an obstacle course ... propped or swollen tarpaulins laid end to end by ministerial forces. Blistered landfills made mountainous.

He heard the music. Or he remembered the music. And smiled as he saw again the single tall mast far out on the sea. Sloping from true to angle and back again like a conductor's baton. His brother had returned.

He felt a tap on his shoulder. It was the Summer Visitor, it surely must be. There was nobody there. But he heard the blue 'train'—evidently now restored to the lower promenade—moving off on its first pleasure trip of a new season. Or a test run, perhaps, because now it was a night land he saw spreading under a black veil of tissue paper across the Bonnyville roofs towards a more clogged and cluttered horizon than the sea's.

Sunny days were just as far away, if not further.

○

Denise Dumond—as the seasons slid by into the aging garb of years—could often be found haunting the customer's catchment area of Robert Smee's fish stall at the entrance to Bonnyville Pier. She had a crush, one she did not admit to herself nor to her best friend, June Derleth. Perhaps June herself was caught up in the same inadmissible crush, although it is difficult to believe they didn't privately talk about it, if in code.

Summer Visitors of even younger ages and persuasions, could also be found uncharacteristically indulging in healthy fish feasts having persuaded their parents or other older escorts to patronise Robert's stall. Indeed, since the clearance of 'the rubbish of dreams' epoch by time-wasters, Summer Visitors no longer came to Bonnyville singly, but now in increasing droves, much to the help of its otherwise insular economy ... putting paid, too, to all the journalistic fantasies of near-collapse of coastal communities that had done a tour of semi-belief in recent years.

The blue 'train' was ever athrob with happy flag-wavers on each of its pointless curvets down the prom and back again. These smiling faces were now known collectively as Day-Trippers. Meantime, young local women like Denise and June often found it difficult to recognise the pigeon-holes wherein they should file the self-nobodies they found extending claw-holds of personality within themselves during the growing-up process. Day-trippers were immune to any benighted features that seemed to be prevalent in coastal communities of Warm England.

Denise was one of the local doctor's daughters, who carried her class as well as her ethnicity with a proud sweep of her mane. She knew her father was central to Bonnyville life. June was nearly in the same class as Denise, her father, Mr Derleth, being one of the town's few traders, who had run a clock and watch shop (recently diversified into much else) in the High Street.

Things got mixed up, concerns at cross-purposes with frivolities, demarcation lines tangled by whatever viewpoints were available at the time any view was taken. Today, for example, Robert Smee had a large catch of snoutfish to purvey. His was a rather loosely-termed 'business'—a makeshift slimy stall or trestle-table which he erected after having himself personally fished the catch in a small boat, between a dinghy and a trawler. He had one male member of staff, who accompanied him and cut incisions into the snouts to make them more presentable on the 'slab', indeed more cosmetically palatable. This other man did not help on the stall itself, for similar reasons. He merely vanished into wherever he had first emerged at the early calling of the ever earlier sun.

Not until recently had Robert been able to fish so openly, but following the lifting of life-style quotas, he could now cast-off with pride into the tissue of lies that dawn prefigured as sunny weather, chasing his own fishtail, as it were, just as monsoons bred off Holland only to emerge without warning here on the North Sea coast of Eastern England. The snoutfish had grown plumper with the changing conditions, so any risks were worth forgetting.

Robert was rather intrigued by the two girls who chatted him up during the stall hours. They looked too young to be out of school. It rather gave him a sense of masculine power but he understood full well how important it was for him to resist temptations in the current climate. He was relieved to be able to deceive himself into believing they were only down here for art lessons—with him and his stall merely unpaid life-models. Ah well, he might need a doctor one day. If not a watch. He looked at his bare wrist. No need to fish further than the topmost tides of timelessness, where there was already plenty to catch without reaching deeper.

○

"The season has already started, with August, its high point, only a few months away. I sit here shaping my own monologue for a wider audience under the illusion that I am simply talking to myself … as time ticks by, evenings draw out and natural auras become more painterly. It remains dark at regular intervals, but night itself shapes itself towards shorter and shorter bites of the luscious light cherry. Given time to measure it.

"I do odd jobs for Robert Smee. Piecework. That's how I've managed to get under a real roof again. (Looks up at the foxed ceiling with a simple prayer for good weather!) Did I actually smile, then?

"You know Smee, of course? He has the eye for the girls. He'll be in a hell of a trouble one day, I reckon. Meanwhile, he's on a crest of a wave, with the over-spawning of the snoutfish. Can be disguised as primest cod with a simple nip and tuck from a gutting-knife. That's my job. And going out at the ever-widening crack of dawn in my all-weather gear upon the high fin-full seas. It makes a man of me. Local economy is served. And thus eventually the Government itself. I sometimes think I know the Prime Minister personally. Most people shout at him from the safety of their TV dinners. I speak to him for real through the 'wireless broadband' of my brain. An extra brain that I sometimes think thinks things I don't. Can say things I can't. No watch and no mobile. But duration flows through my veins with a non-text communication like syrupy captchas.

"The sea's humped with redoubts. Whales or even larger creatures swimming within Warm England's territorial waters, I guess. Some say it's the Government's way of replacing landfills! Smee and I have the Devil's own job navigating.

"At least, Bonnyville keeps its character, even after the school was demolished. No need for a school they said, when nobody any longer spawns themselves back into being. Well, that's the way my strange brain puts it. I don't want to be googled to death, do I? I keep my words ungoogleable. Nobody would google 'ungoogleable' in a month of Sundays, I say!

"Now for the real reason I embarked on this monologue.

"Claura.

"I am now allowed back into *The Sixpenny Queen*, having apologised for my earlier behaviour last Christmas and I suppose getting a job, however unsteady, has helped towards my rehabilitation. I love Claura. Even though she has become matronly, I know where my heart lies. I can still glimpse the svelte figure hidden among the folds of new flesh and the chirpy flirty glances behind the dour frowns. We have a date tomorrow. Our first official date. We're going to the pictures. They've reopened the bingo hall as a cinema on certain days of the week. Culture in a cultural desert. I bet the films are just DVDs, though! Never mind we can re-instate the art of backrow snogging! Did I smile again, then? (Looks towards the ceiling again as the humdrum of rain continues through the shortening night—shortening paradoxically by not sleeping). I wish I could sleep. I was thinking of animals and fish and how they saw their own minds. Perhaps the confusions of sleep and half-forgotten dreams represent a barely comprehensible preview of having a non-human mind should one be reincarnated as an animal or insect. Frightening. The true horror story.

"I wonder what pigs think? Do they believe they can fly?

"Well, with August not so far away again, I wonder whether I shall recognise the Summer Visitor when she arrives disguised within the company of all those other day-trippers flocking off the trains. Perhaps she is not a visitor at all, but here all the time?

"(Looks out the spattered window during the first signs of dawn. Sees a rising hump at sea with a large fat periscope). Laughs. At least I don't have to get up early for work if I never go to sleep."

NOTE: *It is currently considered that Adrian's so-called monologues whenever they occur are apocryphal and will not appear in any final edition of this work.*

○

As the new season picked up its early stride, steamer jaunts were initiated for the first time in the history of Bonnyville. A huge vessel called the 'Glittenburier' was moored at the end of the pier each Sunday and took sight-seers through the Humps as far towards the known horizon as it was possible to go without it becoming a different horizon.

This was a hopping trip, whereby passengers could disembark from time to time at a select few of the newly inhabited Humps, where scientific experiments were now being conducted or observatories set up to examine the night sky without light pollution or landmass interference.

Claura watched the 'Glittenburier' churn along the coast towards the pier's end one particular Sunday morning, its huge funnel belching 'warm-free' fumes like a sick old man smoking a pipe on his back, his flailing arms being paddlewheels transporting him across the sea's upper seabed in slow procession of motion's thought-patterns. She watched it without thinking. There was no need to note its passage with any attention as she was otherwise intent on reaching one of the beach huts for quite a different context.

Her husband had managed to contact her the night before— having evidently escaped from prison. He had stowed himself away in one of the shoreside chalets, but which one was unclear. Her heart was in her mouth, as she had only seen him during formal visiting hours, and even those occasions had grown, in recent years, fewer and fewer. She retained a loyalty to him, despite the way he had behaved to her during their marriage ... whilst also never forgiving (nor understanding) the crime for which he was being punished with a life term. She had not questioned how such a prisoner could have managed to escape. The drive to run towards the beach huts was simply the gut nature of a once pretty now gone-to-seed woman following an unstoppable instinct that was not even her own instinct. And here she was trying to open an ill-painted and evidently locked plank door (to the consternation of nearby day-trippers legitimately opening their own commissioned beach-hut nearby) as the 'Glittenburier' finally moored at the far end of the pier with an audible sky-echoing hoot and hiss. Even the blue 'train' had stopped to watch. But not Claura.

Mr Socrates watched, too. He watched Claura. No longer a teacher, he had taken to mooning about the sea front thinking of new careers he could take. But no new careers would ever come ... certainly in Bonnyville. Except that of unpaid watcher. A watcher of the waves. Having given up any hope of interest in the sight of Claura's skirmishing from hut to hut (although this was a strange occurrence), he walked to the end of the pier to watch the embarkation of the 'Glittenburier'.

Many of the children he had taught—now grown up and attending college a commuting distance away from the town—Palisers and Dumonds alike—were mingling with the day-trippers. Evidently, something they had planned as a Sunday treat preferable to church. Old enough to decide for themselves. He missed them. He had failed to rescue them from life.

He saw that, since the previous voyage, the steamer had acquired a human-sized figurehead of rich but dull marble in imprecise conjoinment with seasoned timber: an embedment at the prow under the bowsprit. A figurehead with feathers ruffled by the wind. An ultramarine effigy.

○

During a seasonal hiatus that might have explained the elastic chronology of events so far, a specific pair of the many off-seaside Humps tapered taller than any others within middle view
… causing Bonnyvilleans and Day-Trippers alike to search some forgotten cultural or race memory for the word or words to describe them in shorthand conversations.

Seahumps or similar words near enough to warrant shakes of the head, indeed *turnings* of the head from even questioning their meanings. It was as if that pair of ever sky-stretching mounds with twirled tops had always been positioned out there towards the horizon: two 'seamarks' to totem childhoods.

Perhaps, all our individual existences (and their progressions) necessarily bear a dual rise amid the many lows, representing the contours of life's audit trail complete with weather fronts and incident-graphs. We would need to re-plot our own paths since birth to prove this hypothesis as a general rule. Death can only come after those two figurative 'seahumps' happen to have formed into a state of psychological as well as biographical geography recognisable as twin peaks.

Peaks are relative to vales, as are piques to veils. Adrian was pricked into thinking—when gazing out at the two major seahumps in question—that they were growing as symbols of his own life, thrusting from the tidal swell's swirling to surround them forever till the planet itself ceased to exist. He and Robert Smee had noticed these particular agglomerations with some consternation as more recent trawling of the sea had resulted (during the current period of continued hiatus) in a diminishing captcha of even undoctored snoutfish.

Robert Smee indeed had gone missing for several days—and Adrian had taken the boat out on his own. But caught nothing at all. He only had one pair of hands. He did not have a fisherman's knack. He simply stared up at the nearest of the 'twin peaks' as it towered into its own self-darkening. And rowed back from its uncanny sense of magnetic entrapment.

Adrian's 'twin peaks' in his own life were represented by rowing stores back and forth to the erstwhile pirate radio-ships and, latterly, rowing for Smee. If they were indeed his dual summits of achievement in hindsight, surely death itself was on the next horizon. He shrugged. He had no time—nor the nous—for such thoughts. He'd simply wait for Smee to return. And Claura to loom large again on a bigger and better horizon he always hoped was just around the corner. Or a bigger and better job—like being in charge of the galley on board the 'Glittenburier'. Wishful thinking. Life never could have three peaks.

○

Paul Derleth squinted through his eye-glass at a watch he was mending. The movement was exquisite. Virtually unstoppable. He would tell the customer that it was beyond repair. Give him a few pounds for it as spare parts. Then auction it in London at an enormous profit.

He then heard the door go 'ding!' It was his daughter June. She was streaming with tears. "Dad! Dad!" "What's the matter?" She was so distressed she could hardly talk. "Denise ... she's been found in the blue train .... dead ... her throat cut."

She screamed hysterically, unstoppably. Unlike Denise Dumond, she needed a doctor.

One night, the Bonnyville residents dreamed they were really trapped day-trippers. Whether this was a single dream shared by each dreamer or a series of separate identical dreams could only have been a question asked by anyone left awake enough to wonder.

The Summer was hot that Summer. It was indeed *that* Summer. You know the one, when all the lawns and park swards were seared yellow, even the compartments of countryside competing to outdo each other with variations on the screaming spectra of rapeseed and baked beaches.

Only the sea remained true to its own description as bleached blue.

And walls were fried like egg-yolk left to harden on plates by lazy washers-up.

At the entrance to the baguette shop near the pier, the building's sandstone was bleached where the shape-sized lintel support itself was now emptied by the same shape that many remembered as being there but not quite what it was.

The boy who had once painted this newly missing 'thing' off-site within Mr Socrates' erstwhile classroom at the demolished Bonnyville junior school walked past. It was impossible to tell whether his eyes shifted to the side surreptitiously to check on the effect of any presence frustrated by the imposition of absence. Inscrutable, as the very notion of perception clouded by mismemory or mistelling.

Other colours invaded the town towards the heart of that summer.

The white of a supermarket's bedraggled biodegradable bags.

The spattered red of the memory sacs. The blood covering the body of Denise Dumond as it swagged between two carriages of the 'train'.

And yes things with intrinsic colours like the blue of not only the 'train' but also the electrical magnetism of the sea mists around the horizon's 'twin peaks'.

The white flesh of the snoutfish on Smee's slab. He had returned to Bonnyville quite as inexplicably as his departure had been full of confident surmising. Adrian was no longer his co-boatman, as Adrian had bigger fish to fry ... on the 'Glittenburier'. Smee fished single-handedly now amid the seahumps. The totems of all modern childhoods. Except there were few such left in the dried out womb of Bonnyville.

The purple of day-trippers' faces pertaining to cardiac arrest should they holiday too conscientiously. Even the Summer Visitor herself bore her own colour. So yellow she couldn't be seen against the grass or beach upon which she alternately sun-bathed.

Finally, the pinkness of a basted, bloated circus tent or loose-strung portakabin in the fleshy shape of a huge creature waddling porkily to its site on the park's yellow sward under the hands of its pitchers and minders. All in church dome hats.

Not a circus tent, in actual fact, as it turned out, but the temporary police HQ for the murder enquiry.

○

Detective Sgt. Gus Hogg stared at his hands. They were the hands of a wonderful human being. Short, squat fingers like teats but sporting elsewhere life-lines a student of palmistry would likely kill for. He then stared up at the slinky hot 'blancmange' of the portakabin's temporary canopy rippling in a rare breeze: temporary prior to someone building a less temporary, yet still temporary, roof. He always thought portakabins were meant to come complete at outset!

"This is a shitting hellhole!" he shouted into his over-sized walkie talkie.

The heat was not filtered out by the 'blancmange' (if that was what it was): a cooling gel steeped into the canopy's weave with a process of overnight marinade by cold storage. But nothing could cope with this particular August's sweltering.

"And the town's full of crones and creeps and tattooed bleeders on the beach and shitting sea-gulls! How am I supposed to pin anything on anybody when half the population doesn't even live here and have come just to see the shitting sea! Beats me why anyone would want to come as near as twenty thousand shitting miles of this place!"

Whoever was at the other end of this conversation squeaked inarticulately—as heard by Constable Milly Mauve when she arrived with a sheaf of papers from another part of the huge complex that constituted the 'portakabin'.

"A list of the suspects here, sir," she said, pinching her own bum in an absent-minded attempt to ward off the same sexual harassment from anyone else. A lesson in psychological policing. She was horrified by Hogg's nasal cavities and residual contents following a recent sneeze.

○

The Summer Visitor unwound herself from the colour-trap against which backdrop she had been painted into a corner of the beach … now revealing a yellow-stained ghost standing naked and vulnerable. Cold despite the heat. Another murder victim come to haunt its own murder. Not a re-enactment as such but a ceremonial purging of a crime by disguising, in hindsight, its violence with a different slow-motion déjà-vu: simply an unfortunate accident.

She did no want to waste police time. She knew—even as a ghost—that her own murder was insoluble. So why not make it an accident under a scribble of wings created by the bird-crumb man all those many months before? The police would have their work cut out simply solving the potentially soluble crime of Denise Dumond's murder. A murder worth its salt.

The Summer Visitor, on the other hand, had simply fallen from a crashing jet liner. Or clambered from the sea as the sole survivor—only to die on the beach. Or glided as a gradually solidifying corpse upon the sound-waves of the Government's explosive testing from across the wide estuary. A Fortean phenomenon. Or was just a day-tripper who had died a natural purple-faced death, turned yellow by decay.

Whatever the case, the Summer Visitor perhaps instinctively needed that buffoon Det. Sgt. Hogg to concentrate his limited resources within his 'pink balloon' on a more worthwhile murder. One that would save future girls like Miss Dumond (she thought) from lethal interference by internet groomers such as Charles Paliser. But ghosts were not omniscient. Not even any ability to be a detective. They had no ability beyond that of subsisting beyond death. That took all their energy.

The yellow ghost returned to its Summer camouflage as a supine sun-bather, refortifying her strength against death's reclamation of her non-existence.

A lady with wide hips waddled by with two laden supermarket bags. She saw only real live people on the beach. Only day-trippers with tattoos and silly sunhats. Not even a single long-term Summer Visitor among them. No wonder she had given up running a bed-and-breakfast for long-stays at Bonnyville. Nobody seemed to want to remain overnight any more. Not like the good old days of Variety Shows and ballroom dancing. And with those thoughts, she struggled on to the corner shop for her husband's liquorice whips. Tesco didn't stock them.

Every cloud has a gold lining. It was the beginning of the frost again in the ever-turning movement of each season's watch. Adrian's stream of pee steamed like dry ice as it gushed fulsomely into the lavatory bowl, one that was uncommonly large with seemingly a deep lake of blue water at the bottom gradually being stained yellow by Adrian's generous flow. He had been drinking. This was a seasonal public lavatory still carelessly left open by Bonnyville Council after the departure of the day-trippers: a communal trough that drunken men often circled with equally generous flows of idle chatter between them. But tonight Adrian was on his own, on shore leave from the 'Glittenburier'. He called it shore leave. He had simply been laid off with the end of the season.

He staggered through the night in search of the blue train's off-season parking place close by which he believed Claura to live. *The Sixpenny Queen* had been turned into a ghost train. Old pubs were either knocked down or became supermarkets, so *The Sixpenny Queen* was relatively lucky to remain a haunt for those wanting to be scared out of being scared. Much like Adrian's own diary ready for any newspaper to pay him millions for his story of purge and power, or he hoped so under another bout of wishfulness. An embarrassment to his family, with all of the Palisers no doubt tonight dining at the Prime Minister's official residence Chequers … except for a black sheep like Adrian.

He had been at sea so long his staggering was twofold. He saw the shimmering shadow of a huge inflated pig. Shaped from a cellophane sea. He knew he was drunk, but surely drinking was simply a way to diminish imagination, not enhance it.

He was pleased to see the Apocryphan was back in position within the frame of the baguette shop's doorway. Blue disinfectant in its eyes.

○

Paul Derleth squinted at the innards of a clock. A cheep-chiming clock that combined—when working properly—the sound of a babbling brook with the traditional rhythm of a woodpecker disguised as the first cuckoo of Spring to mark each passing nostalgia for each passing hour.

He was hounded by ruthless spivs from London for bending bent deals even further than the tightest watch spring. They had obviously thought his daughter June was really her friend Denise Dumond. On that deadly night before the Summer. He shrugged. Mistaken identity. As long as he kept his own nose clean.

At least the policeman in charge of the enquiry had an even bigger nose in his own trough for enquiries into identities to last beyond the faces on the hidden faces of a hand of playing-cards. And Paul Derleth certainly kept his own cards close to his chest.

○

Tick tock. Tick tock. Doctor Dumond listened to the prone body of Mr Socrates on the examination couch. Life for the doctor had to go on since the brutal murder of his daughter Denise. His ears squinted to pick up the sound waves via the stethoscope … and he thought he heard her tiny screams inside the chest wallful of wheezing lungs. Dr Dumond was no midwife, but he hoped to induce his patient into coughing up a knot of incriminating phlegm that contained a hairball from Denise's hair to pass to the policeman in the pink portakabin.

As well as having her throat cut, forensic evidence in the ensuing months and years had indicated that parts of Denise had also been eaten by the murderer. Only a doctor could make indigestion an ingredient of a whodunnit. Not that this was an easy read. Not even a work of detective fiction at all.

Imagination could thrive in real life, imagination could *become* real life, imagination could indeed enhance boring truth into a powerhouse of wild visions rather than into its more normal defaulting towards blank walls, with or without alcohol … or the disinfectant of disbelief.

Constable Milly Mauve started by following various leads that eventually led to a middle-aging Claura Gill.

Everyone who had investigated the murder of Denise Dumond over the years had automatically assumed it had been carried out by a ravening male. The Augusthog, as the pink blancmange portakabin was called in 'honour' of its encroaching permanence to replace the crumbling war memorial as a landmark for approaching boats, was full of backbiting, crudity, sexism, racism and sheer gratuitous spite. Many a holidaymaker had been banged up there simply because they had started singing out of tune in a pub or missing their step during a foxtrot. Milly, however, never lost the plot quite so completely as the clueless male officers she saw around her in the portakabin. She was so self-subsumed she could actually empathise with the most unlikely motives. Including affection-subterfuge or blame-transference or paradox-immersion or sexual envy across and between genders.

A male murderer, Milly was convinced, would never have preferred eating the body without first corrupting it with the effects of his lust. And after several months of paperwork crossing the corridors of the Augusthog, it had been discovered that Denise's body, short of the bits missing through eating, was otherwise intact.

Meanwhile, over the years, Milly watched Claura standing on several separate occasions at the end of the pier gazing towards the sea-humps and the electrical storms shorting between the two main dumpy 'earths' that the erstwhile peaks had become by dint of heavenly erosion. As if Claura were expecting a loved one to return from his sojourn abroad, sailing between those very humps' shifting shapes. A bastard of a man, resurrected from drowning, one who had once ill-treated Claura, the simple-minded Claura who had in turn loved him with unrequited passion, thus losing her heart to him when it was taken aboard his body during a devilmaycare attempt to emulate the Flying Dutchman upon the High Seas. A Romance of adventure and derring-do.

So Milly deduced that Claura had killed Denise Dumond by misplaced role-playing, in vicarious hope that it was the work of the love-rat who had secretly returned to Bonnyville by the effect of there having been such a suitable crime perpetrated in Bonnyville at all. So, by Claura initiating the need for a murder hunt, Milly was convinced that Claura was convinced the culprit (whom she now carried within her as he had once carried her within him) would be excised from her body and reunited within her arms, as a villain made manifest by her own villainy. A convoluted motive to flesh out Claura's love-rat lover in her own shape that made sense only to women police officers like Milly. Cannibalism had been the icing on the cake. Or simply the clincher to complete the circle. It all made sense to Milly. If not to Claura Gill herself who continued to gaze out to sea for many more years following the actual murder—now intent on marrying the first-comer between the humps, whoever it was, love-rat or handsome French Lieutenant or black-eyed pirate or even Father Christmas.

Milly Mauve, meanwhile, never gave up hope of nailing the crime to its mast. Ever on the watch itself for others watching.

Robert Smee's Fish Stall had only one customer … and only one fish. Whether the single fish was the residue of an earlier rush by Autumn Locals to shop for fish before another storm came or simply just the one and only fish he'd fished that morning. Indeed, the only customer, when scrutinised more closely, was not really a customer at all but Adrian after his old job back as Smee's boatman.

"Sorry, mate," said Smee, "but you can see how things are."
He indicated the snoutless flesh-meagre skeleton that looked as
if it had been dragged through a cat backwards. Nevertheless, it
still flipped slightly on the slimy wooden trestle using its fins as
twitchy re-beginnings in the life cycle.

"It'll be nice to join up again," said Adrian, "even if you don't
pay me until we find fish again."

"We won't find fish again. The only fish left are those pre-
packed at Tesco." There were discernible tears in Smee's eyes. "But
I don't sleep very well and I keep thinking too deep about things.
Things that keep coming back. Things I don't want to remember.
And I do like your company, mate. It takes my mind off things—
your jokes. Maybe we'll catch fish again, OK. Maybe also we can
go out together now and again, after all. See how it goes, as you
say. The dinghy's too big for one."

"Yes, yes, that would be really good." As he spoke, Adrian
gazed towards the top of the foreshortened War Memorial, where
he imagined three people poised to jump, one as blue as the
Summer sky had once been, invisible then … till now gloom had
underpinned its weight of colour as a real thing. Also a crippled
old soldier. (How had a crippled old soldier got up there?) And
Claura was there, it seemed, eager for a better view of the 'sea'
from there than that from the now hump-surrounded pier.

Indeed the 'sea' was now a near complete mass of conjoining
land-humps. All this talk of fishing was simply that … talk. The
only fish on the trestle was not only the only fish today but the last
ever fish in the world, perhaps. Tesco notwithstanding. It twitched
for its own last time and died. Ready for eating. Ready for choking
upon.

Adrian looked slightly more inland beyond the rooftops and
saw the pink hard-swelling tent-top of the Augusthog. Bright
shimmering 'blancmange', despite the gloom that surrounded it.
Or, rather, because of it. Adrian knew things were paradoxes or
they could not be things at all. A truism to say that. But only a

49

truism because it was a paradox first and foremost and not obvious at all. It all made sense. Like the Government's recently launched pirate radio ship (the Glittenburier) now perched high-and-dry on the mud-flats like the re-beginnings of Mast-Henge ... at a mooring where the 'twin peaks' had once distantly totemed many childhoods. A Government displaced. A Government fighting anarchy from its own non-territorial base of anarchy.

It was simply, however, a ghost ship. The Flying Dutchman becalmed upon its own self-created Sargasso Sea.

○

As Smee dragged the early broken morning to his dinghy via the edge where the sea's edge used to be, he spotted Adrian coming towards him from the promenade, complete with sensible sou'wester and water-resistant galoshes. Upon arrival, the newcomer, wordless in face of wordlessness, stooped to help pull the dinghy further towards where the sea used to be. Pulled and dragged across the many runnels and sand-ribs that final sad tides as sculptors of geography had left. Through more significant puddles that would have been too shallow for any self-respecting lavatory-bowl or soup tureen. Ever-pulling. Ever-dragging. Between the humps as well as across them in desperate search for at least a smidgen of sea to fish. Until the two men and the dinghy reached the site of the twin totems—now flattened mud-flats, at least shaped like sea, if not constituted of it.

Both men, in dour mood, returned their gazes towards the coast whence they'd pulled and dragged the dinghy ... and they forthwith traced Bonnyville's skyline with careless pencils of memory. There the spinnakered 'Augusthog'—a new artistic challenge as if from Mr Socrates' ancient art class in Bonnyville's late lamented schoolhouse—became a mighty bloated blood-vessel sailing with ease across the land toward them. Frictionless as fiction. A vision of a painting. A motion-filled painting of an aviational 'porco rosso' turned marine with the ease if not slowness of Darwinian evolution: scaled beyond the scale of even the wildest artistic imagination. Reality made art, art made reality, in a symbiosis or synergy of both.

○

Charlie Bubbles stared through the studio cockpit of the makeshift radio station installed upon the cruise paddle-steamer 'Glittenburier'. As a record spun to a close, he leant towards the microphone...

"Hiya, Gals and Guys, things are remarkably rock steady on the North Sea today. Just looking at my Bulova Watch, I see it is indeed time here on Radio Teacutter to give you the weather forecast for your neck of the woods..."

His mock drawl came to a sudden halt. Across the brown-sludge bay he spotted approaching the imposing sight of a huge grounded air-ship, pink cannons spiking the portholes like they meant business.

○

When Dr Laurence Dumond looked at the wounds on Claura Gill's body, he did wonder, at first, whether she was already dead. But somehow he knew that—without needing a doctor's skill to fathom such matters—corpses do not usually have wounds that continue bleeding so generously. Parts of the body's upholstery were missing where these wounds met flesh at raw-edged encounters of violence with long-term growth as a woman. The bones suddenly moved, a ratchet twist or twitch, as if the bones themselves regained consciousness intermittently ... a series of startled awakenings. The scenario—at least up to that final point—reminded the doctor of a similar nightmare, when one of his own daughters had been brought into his surgery's consulting room all those years before. In many ways, he claimed 'surgery' was a misnomer. And there had never been an A & E in Bonnyville. Even in the heyday of the NHS.

In the distance, he heard civil war turn global in explosive warmth.

○

The man with no name heard the very same dull rumbles shake the floorboards, sound-cracking the dormer's flat roof together with an instinctive sense of a slight re-positioning from the eaves-cupboards around him. He heard his wife heavily moving about downstairs, to which he had ascribed the vibrations. A huge pink lady.

He chewed ruminatively on the end of a twine of liquorice. He proceeded to slap his thighs rhythmically with a bare hand. Then sipped at a shallow glass of Babycham.

○

As the very same rumbles took their inevitable path of vibration across Bonnyville, the watchmaker squinted at the diversification of his own glass eye as he prodded it with a tiny screwdriver. His daughter June was in the shop downstairs serving someone. He was in hiding upstairs to avoid protection. He had originally wanted to close his business down, especially as the passing trade no longer passed.

With his other eye, he swung a telescope's view through the sweeping angle of his bedroom's bay window. He lived in time's past. The sea was a rich blue, with waves of light glinting off his watch face. Two huge indistinguishable vessels of furnished residue became breeze-blocks upon the horizon, as the floating current brought them together and then apart at each swell of alternate whim.

He took long glance from the mysteries of reality outside and gingerly pulled open the drawer of his desk where within sat several ostensibly incomplete repairs of complex timepieces, lucky if they ticked at all. Using large tweezers, he carefully extracted a miniature apocryphan of blue ormolu from a craftily positioned refraction stand and inserted it with righteous incidence within the contents of the drawer, as if it were to be the intrinsic part of a communal movement provided for some intricately age-perfected timepiece, a timepiece made from several broken ones.

○

The blue cover says 'Apocryfan'. Surely that's a mistake for 'Apocryphan'. I prod it with my screwdriver, examining it through the eye-glass. I am sure I am dreaming. The book was not on my desk when I was awake. It may have been in one of the drawers but, if it was, I'm sure I didn't put it there. My daughter may have put it there, hoping I'd pick it out to see it working. Books can work like osmosis. She's always deep into books, absorbed by reading, doubly sure that she drains time to its dregs. I dream the book is not bound but made inside from a series of loose-leaved pages or cards, with two-headed pictures of a stylised royal family. Fannable by Duchess Guermantes in Proust wanting to cool her fevered brow. I lift the front board cover with the end of my screwdriver. Bits and pieces of human body inside for dealing with which I reach for my middle-sized tweezers. Nature study was always Mr Socrates' forte when a teacher. I hope I am not him.

○

Adrian dragged himself from off the bars of the dream's drain, as the dream itself flowed away into the communal sewage system of Bonnyville's madness. Not only dreaming of the Apocryphan but also dreaming that he, Adrian, was someone else dreaming of someone else dreaming the dream made the dream far more frightening, far more memorable upon waking ... cloying his mood for the rest of the day as he wrestled Smee's dinghy once again across the sealess wastes of Bonnyville Bay in search of the world's final fish.

Only yesterday, his brother Charlie Bubbles (aka Paliser) had been taken off the 'Glittenburier' by a floating horde of policemen. He had been charged with the murder of Denise Dumond and of the mutilation of Claura Gill. Charlie was now being held on board the police vessel by Det. Supt. Hogg for further questioning. The actual mechanics of this arrest, including the subsequent anchoring of the police vessel nearby, had all happened without assistance from the lubrication of dream, but it had happened nevertheless, against the odds, under the auspices of a new Terrorism Act put into place by anti-Government forces. Nobody any longer blamed Mankind for global terrorism, as Nature itself had become the prime suspect, Nature having created Mankind in the first place. Murders and mutilations were simply sideshows and anybody arrested were not arrested for these crimes themselves but for being clowns of a deeper motive that Nature had got jerking like puppets in its cause. Just a means for cosmic slimming. To chill the buds of global warming. Double bluffs, if not triple.

"Do you think the sea will ever return?" asked Adrian absent-mindedly as he faced Smee across the rowlocks of the dinghy. Tonight Adrian was due to visit Claura in hospital a journey away. They had renewed romance between them. Things were not wholly bad.

"The sea never went away," was the careless reply, interrupting Adrian's revery. Smee wasn't intelligent enough to give such an answer. He simply smiled at an inbuilt wisdom that betrayed his own unthinking alliance with Nature. The vision in his head was of higher tides and eroded coasts. Who could say whether *that* vision was less real than the real one around them of sealess wastes?

They shook hands across the dinghy before, with initial positive anticipation, Smee stooped and picked up, from between two sand-ribs, what looked like a pink human foot with only four toes.

Milton Keynes UK
Ingram Content Group UK Ltd.
UKHW030009090924
447944UK00004B/11/J

9 781913 766184